E
SAN

Sanderson, Ruth. *c.1*

The twelve dancing
princesses

The Twelve Dancing Princesses

RETOLD AND
ILLUSTRATED BY
RUTH SANDERSON

LITTLE, BROWN AND COMPANY
BOSTON TORONTO LONDON

First edition

The text for *The Twelve Dancing Princesses*
was retold from the Brothers Grimm.

Paintings done in oil on canvas

Calligraphy by Jeanyee Wong

Library of Congress Cataloging-in-Publication Data

Sanderson, Ruth.
    The twelve dancing princesses / retold and illustrated by Ruth
Sanderson.
        p.   cm.
    Summary: Retells the tale of twelve princesses who dance secretly
all night long and how their secret is eventually discovered.
    ISBN 0-316-77017-5
    [1. Fairy tales. 2. Folklore — Germany.] I. Title. II. Title:
12 dancing princesses.
PZ8.S253Tw 1990
398.2′1′0943 — dc19
[E]   88-28637
                                                                        CIP
                                                                        AC

10 9 8 7 6 5 4 3 2 1

WOR

Published simultaneously in Canada
by Little, Brown & Company (Canada) Limited

Printed in the United States of America

To Maria

Special thanks to Nan Hurlburt
for her costumes and her knowledge about
fifteenth-century dancing.

nce upon a time a king had twelve daughters, each one more beautiful than the last. The twelve princesses slept in twelve beds, all in one enormous room. When they went to bed, their door was locked with triple bolts. Every morning, though, their shoes were found to be quite worn through, as if they had been danced in all night long. When the king asked the princesses what they did at night, their only reply was that they slept. Yet their shoes could not have worn *themselves* out!

At last the king proclaimed to all the land that if any young man could discover the secret of his daughters' worn-out shoes, he would be allowed to choose one of the princesses for his bride.

It was not long before a king's son came to try his luck. He was welcomed into the palace, and in the evening he was taken to a small chamber next to the princesses' room. The door between the two rooms was left ajar so that nothing would happen without his hearing it. In the morning, however, the mystery remained unsolved. The twelve pairs of shoes had once again been worn through, and the prince himself had disappeared. This same fate befell the many princes who followed.

Now it happened that a young commoner named Michael had been traveling throughout the country, seeking his fortune. One hot midday he was sleeping under the shade of a tree. When he opened his eyes, an old woman was watching him from the road.

"Where are you bound this day, my son?" asked the woman.

"I am passing through this land looking for work," said Michael, "and I have heard of the mystery of the princesses' worn-out shoes. I should like to find out their secret; perhaps I might win one of them for my bride."

"Well," said the woman, "I have heard that the gardener at the castle needs a helper. As for the princesses' secret, if you bide your time and use your wits, you just might have more success than the rest."

Then she took a cloak out of her bag and handed it to him, saying, "This cloak will cause you to become invisible, and you will be able to follow the princesses wherever they go." Michael was pleased at his good fortune. He thanked the wise woman and set off at once for the castle.

When he got there, Michael went straight to the gardener to offer his services. The gardener did indeed need a helper, and he agreed to take Michael on.

Michael's first task was to give a bouquet to each of the princesses as she came out onto the terrace in the early afternoon. All of the sisters took the flowers without even glancing at the lad, except for the youngest, Lina. She stared admiringly at him and exclaimed, "Oh, how pretty he is — our new flower boy!"

Her sisters burst out laughing, and the eldest pointed out that a princess ought never to lower herself by looking at an ordinary garden boy.

The sweet face of the youngest princess inspired Michael to try his luck with the test that very night. As a commoner, he dared not go openly to the king, so he decided to use the magic cloak.

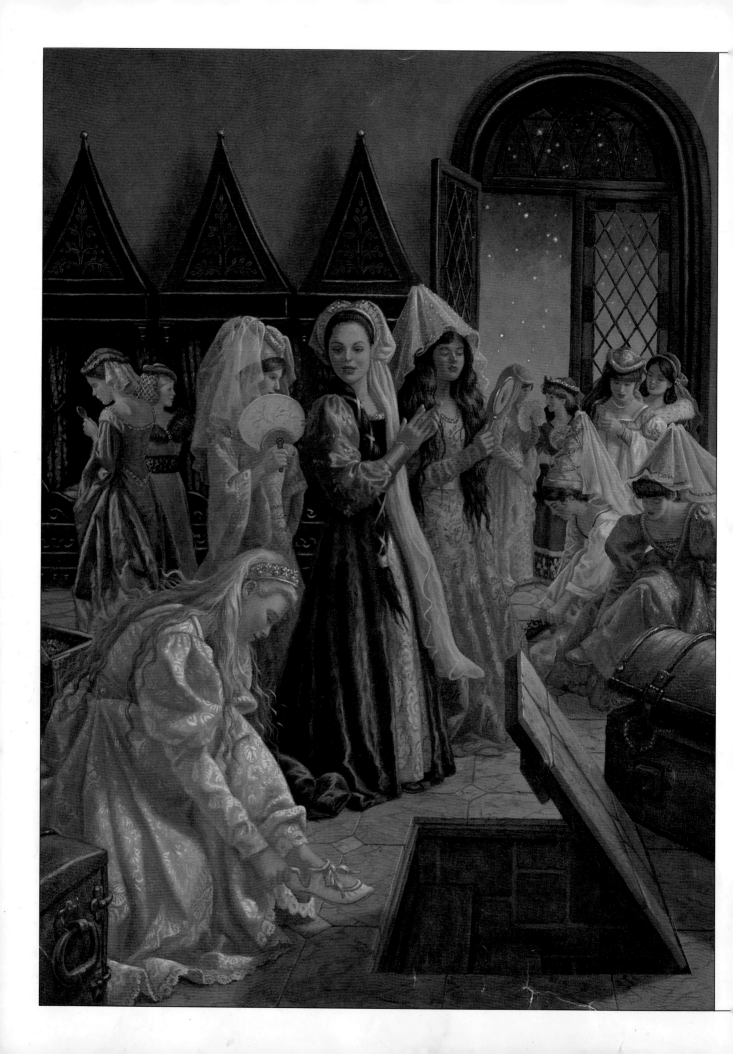

When the princesses went upstairs to bed, Michael followed them silently and hid under one of the twelve beds. As soon as the bolts were slid into the locks, the princesses began to open wardrobes and chests. They chattered and laughed with pleasure as they got dressed in their most beautiful gowns. By the time Michael finally dared to peep out, they were putting on new satin dancing shoes. The eldest then said, "Be quick, sisters — our partners will be impatient." She clapped her hands three times, and a trap door opened in the floor. All the princesses disappeared down a hidden staircase, and Michael hastily followed, invisible in his magic cloak.

Down, down, down they went, until at last they reached a small chamber whose door was fastened only with a latch. As Lina was going down the last few steps, Michael carelessly stepped on her dress.

"What's that?" cried the youngest princess. "Who is holding my dress?"

"Don't be so foolish," said the eldest. "Your dress must be caught on a nail." Lina took a last look up the empty staircase and followed her sisters through the door.

The princesses hurried down a lamp-lit path. It led into a beautiful wood, where the leaves on the trees were spangled with silver. Next they passed into another wood, where the leaves were sprinkled with gold. The sisters

chattered to each other excitedly, all except Lina, who was silent and uneasy. Finally the princesses crossed a third wood, where the leaves glittered with diamonds that sparkled in the night.

They soon came to a large lake. On the shore of the lake were twelve white boats shaped like swans. Twelve princes waited on the shore to help the princesses into the boats.

After Lina entered the last boat, Michael slipped in behind her. The twelve princes took the oars, and the boats glided over the water. Lina's boat, however, was far heavier than the others and so lagged behind.

"We never went so slowly before," said Lina. "What can be the reason?"

"I assure you, I do not know," answered the prince. "I am rowing as hard as I can."

On the other side of the lake Michael saw a magnificent palace like none he had ever seen or imagined. It was splendidly lit, and lively music sounded from within. In a moment the boats landed before it. The princes gave their arms to the princesses and escorted them into the palace.

Michael hid in a corner and admired the grace and beauty of all the princesses. Some were fair, some were dark, but the one whom the garden boy thought the most fascinating was the princess Lina. Her long silken hair flowed around her as she danced with her partner. Her cheeks were flushed, and her eyes sparkled. It was plain that she loved dancing more than anything else.

Michael envied her dancing partner, but in fact he had little cause to be jealous. For these young men were really the princes who had tried to learn the princesses' secret. The eldest princess had given all of them in turn a drink that had frozen their hearts and left them nothing but the love of dancing.

It was almost dawn when the shoes of the princesses were worn through. A lavish supper was then served, after which the dancers returned to the boats.

Again they passed through the wood with the diamond-strewn leaves, the wood with the gold-sprinkled leaves, and the wood with the silver-spangled leaves. Michael broke off a small silver branch as proof of what he had seen.

Lina turned her head at the sound of the branch breaking. "What was that noise?" she asked.

"It was nothing," replied her eldest sister. "It must have been an animal scurrying to its home."

While she was speaking, Michael managed to slip in front of the twelve sisters, and he reached the princesses' room first. He flung open a window and slid down the stout vine that climbed the castle wall. The sun was just beginning to rise, so he went to the garden to do his day's work.

That afternoon, when he was arranging the princesses' bouquets, Michael hid the branch with the silver-spangled leaves in the flowers for Lina. When she discovered it, the princess was much surprised. Nevertheless, she said nothing to her sisters about it.

That evening the twelve sisters again went to the ball. Once again Michael followed them and crossed the lake in Lina's boat. This time the prince complained that the boat seemed heavier than usual.

"It must be the heat," said Lina. "I, too, have been feeling quite warm."

During the dancing she looked everywhere for the garden boy, but not once did she catch a glimpse of him.

On the way back, Michael broke a branch from the wood with the gold-sprinkled leaves. This time the eldest princess heard the snap of the branch.

"It was nothing," said Lina, "just an animal scurrying to its home."

The next afternoon Lina found the branch with the gold-sprinkled leaves in her bouquet. After her sisters went back inside, Lina remained behind and went over to the garden boy.

"Where did this branch come from?" she asked him.

"Your Highness knows well enough," Michael replied.

"So you have followed us?"

"Yes, Princess."

"We never saw you. How did you manage it?"

"I hid myself," Michael answered.

Lina was silent a moment, and then she said, "Now that you know our secret, you must keep it!" She threw down a purse of gold. "Here is the reward for your silence."

Michael walked away without picking up the purse.

For three nights Lina neither saw nor heard anything unusual. On the fourth night, however, she heard a rustling in the wood with the diamond-strewn leaves. The next afternoon her bouquet contained a branch from that wood.

She took Michael aside and said to him curtly, "You know what my father has promised to pay for our secret?"

"I do know, Princess," answered Michael.

"Do you intend to tell him?"

"No, I don't."

"Why not?" Lina asked.

But Michael was silent.

Lina's sisters had seen her talking to the garden boy. They teased her, saying, "Why don't you marry him? You could become a gardener, too, and help him bring our bouquets every day." Their teasing greatly disturbed Lina, and when they returned to the castle she told her eldest sister everything.

"What!" her sister said. "How could you wait so long to tell me! We must be rid of him at once."

"How?"

"Why, by having him thrown into the dungeon, of course."

Lina persuaded her sister to discuss the matter with their other ten sisters. They all agreed with the eldest that Michael should be put in the dungeon.

Lina surprised them all by declaring that if they harmed Michael in any way, she would tell their father the secret of their worn-out shoes.

So they decided to ask Michael to come with them to the ball. At the end of the banquet they would offer him the drink that would enchant him like the other young men.

Now, Michael had been working outside the window and had overheard the princesses' plan. He resolved to risk everything and try to win Lina's heart that night. If necessary, he would take the drink and sacrifice himself for the one he loved.

Upon returning to his room, Michael found an invitation to that evening's ball pinned to a suit of fine clothes.

The twelve princesses went up to bed, and Michael followed, wearing the invisible cloak over his finery. This time he did not cross the lake in Lina's boat. Instead, he ran ahead through the woods and entered the eldest sister's boat. Arriving first at the palace, Michael hid the cloak in the bushes and, as if by magic, appeared at the door to greet the princesses.

During the evening Michael danced with each princess in turn. They were

all delighted with his charm and grace. At last the time came for him to dance with Lina. He found her the best partner in the world, though her smile seemed almost sad.

When the princesses' dancing shoes were worn through, the music stopped. All the dancers sat down at the banquet table. Michael was seated at the head, as the guest of honor. On either side sat Lina and the eldest sister.

Delicious food and drink were then served, and the sisters flattered Michael with compliments. When everyone had finished eating, the eldest princess made a sign. A page brought in a large silver cup and offered it to the garden boy.

Michael took a last look at the youngest princess. He accepted the cup and raised it to his lips.

"Don't drink it," Lina cried out suddenly. "I would rather be a gardener's wife!"

At once Michael threw the contents of the cup onto the floor behind him. He knelt at Lina's feet and kissed her hand. All of the princes were freed from the enchantment and fell on their knees before the princesses. The spell was broken.

Led by Michael and Lina, everyone boarded the boats to cross the lake. For the last time they passed through the three beautiful woods. When they had all gone through the door of the underground passage, a great rumbling noise rose up, as if the enchanted palace were tumbling to the ground.

Michael and the twelve princesses went straight to the king, who was eating breakfast in his chambers. The king was surprised to see his twelve daughters led by the garden boy. Michael held out the silver cup and revealed the secret of the worn-out dancing shoes.

"Is this true?" the king asked his daughters, for he was a man who did not believe in magic cloaks or enchanted castles.

The twelve princesses reluctantly admitted to their father that Michael spoke the truth.

"Very well," said the king, amazed by Michael's cleverness. "You may choose whichever princess you prefer."

"My choice is already made," Michael replied as he held out his hand to Lina, the youngest princess.

The wedding was held the very next day, and the king declared that when he died Michael would inherit the kingdom. So Lina did not become a gardener's wife, after all. Instead, one day Michael would be king.